Billy's Big-Boy Bed

Phyllis Limbacher Tildes

Whispering Coyote
A Charlesbridge Imprint

For Marta Limbacher, with love

With special thanks to my editors, Yolanda LeRoy and Lisa Laird,
and to young John Patrick Mooney,
who was a great inspiration

2003 first paperback edition
Text and illustrations copyright © 2002 by Phyllis Limbacher Tildes

Published by Charlesbridge
85 Main Street, Watertown, MA 02472
(617) 926-0329
www.charlesbridge.com

Library of Congress Cataloging-in-Publication Data
Tildes, Phyllis Limbacher.
Billy's big-boy bed / Phyllis Limbacher Tildes.
p. cm.
Summary: As Billy gets too big for his crib, his parents buy him a new bed, but Billy is not sure
he is ready for the change, until his favorite teddy bear ends up sleeping in the new bed.
ISBN 1-57091-475-3 (reinforced for library use)
ISBN 1-57091-606-3 (softcover)
[1. Beds—Fiction. 2. Growth—Fiction.] I. Title.
PZ7.T4559 Bi 2002
[E]—dc21   2001023548

Printed in Hong Kong
(hc) 10 9 8 7 6 5 4 3 2 1
(sc) 10 9 8 7 6 5 4 3 2 1

Illustrations done in watercolor on Strathmore 4-ply illustration paper
Display type and text type set in Stone Sans
Printed and bound by Toppan Printing Company, Hong Kong
Production supervision by *The Kids at Our House*
Designed by Phyllis Limbacher Tildes

Billy was getting big.
His clothes were too small.
His shoes were too tight.

Even his crib was too crowded for Billy and
all his bears.
"I think it's time you got a big-boy bed,"
said Billy's mother.

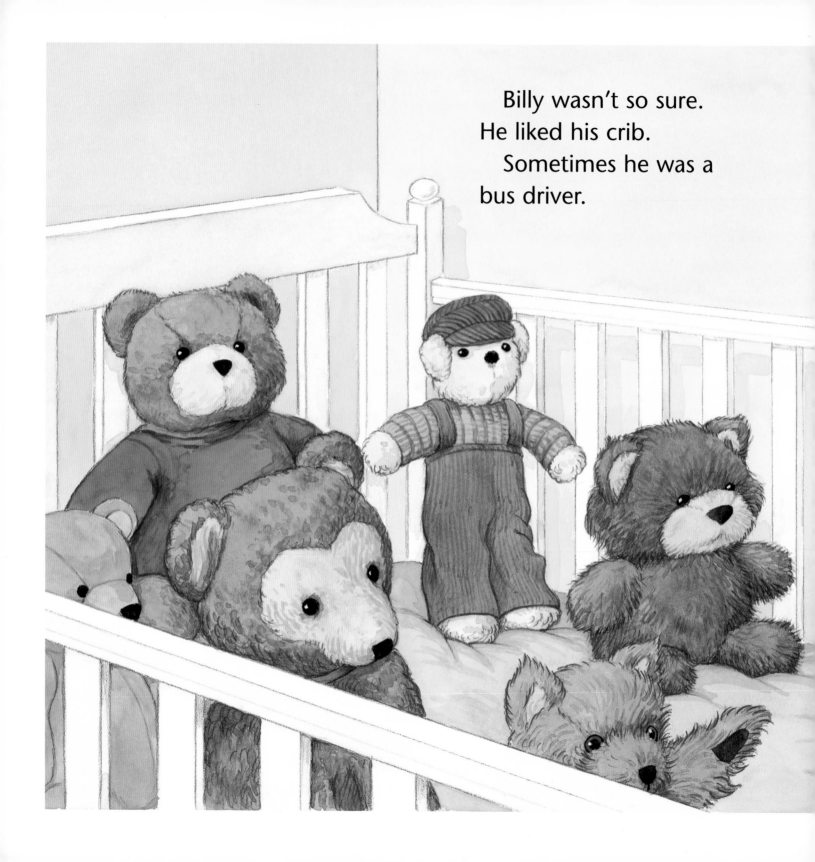

Billy wasn't so sure.
He liked his crib.
Sometimes he was a
bus driver.

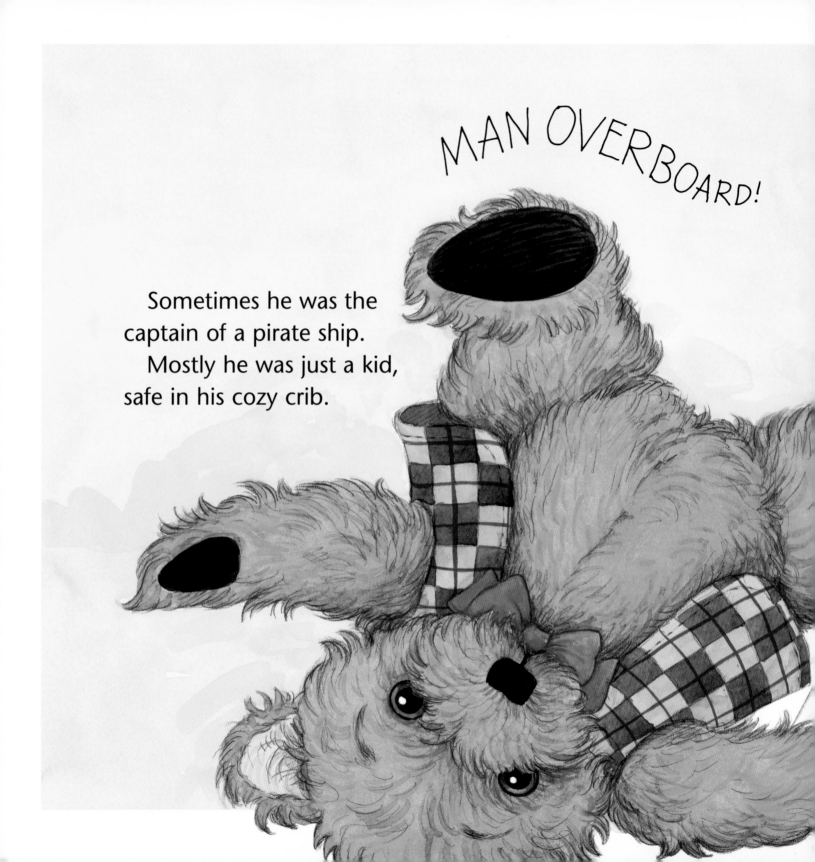

MAN OVERBOARD!

Sometimes he was the captain of a pirate ship. Mostly he was just a kid, safe in his cozy crib.

A few days later Billy's mother and father took
him to a furniture store.

There were king-size beds to lie on.

There were queen-size beds to roll on.

There were twin-size beds
to bounce on.

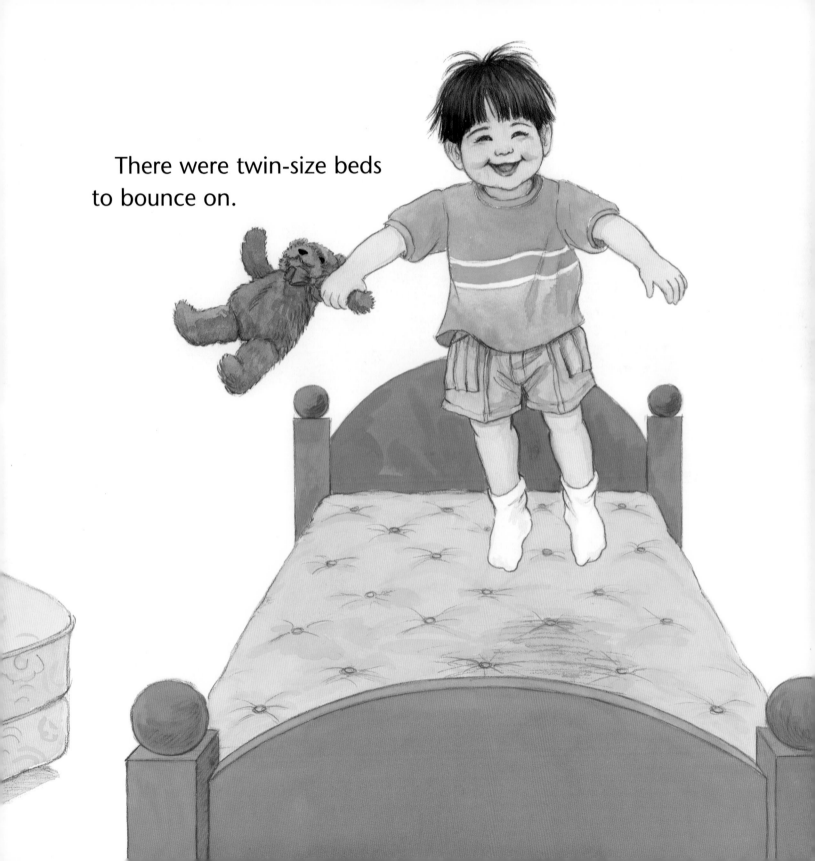

One of the beds even had three big drawers below.
Billy opened and closed each one. Fuzz, Billy's favorite
teddy bear, liked the drawers a lot.

The salesman asked Billy if he liked the big-boy bed.
Billy hugged his father's leg and wouldn't answer. The
grown-ups talked together while Billy and Fuzz
whispered to each other.

The very next day a truck pulled up
to Billy's house. Two men lugged huge
boxes and a mattress into the house
and up to Billy's bedroom.

"This looks like a big-boy bed. Are you sure it's for you?" asked one of the men, chuckling.

"I *am* a big boy!" insisted Billy.

The men pushed Billy's crib across the room, put the new bed together, and left.

Billy watched his mother put new sheets and a puffy quilt on the new bed.

"Would you like to put all your bears on the bed?" she asked.

"No. Just this one," he replied.

Billy tossed his newest bear onto the big bed. He took Fuzz and went outside to play.

At bedtime, Billy climbed into his crib
and turned his back to the new bed. His
parents smiled and said that was fine.

Billy peeked over his shoulder at the bed. In the glow of the night-light, the new bed looked like a gigantic monster lurking in the dark. Billy squeezed his eyes shut and hugged Fuzz. It took him a long time to fall asleep.

In the bright morning light Billy and Fuzz romped on
top of the puffy quilt.

Later in the day Billy put some of his toys and clothes
in the drawers under the big bed.

At bedtime he placed two more bears on top.

"Come on, Billy, why don't you try your new bed tonight?" suggested his father.

Billy shook his head no. His parents kissed him good night and left the room. From his crib he could see three friendly, furry faces looking back at him.

On the third night Billy placed all his bears, except Fuzz, on the new bed.

"Shall we read your bears a story tonight?" asked his mother.

Billy got one of his favorite books and climbed on top of the new bed for story time. Soon his bears were very sleepy.

"You look so comfy in this nice big bed, Billy," his mother said.

At that, Billy bolted out of the bed and climbed back into the crib with Fuzz. Billy's father came to say good night.

"Looks to me like Billy's going to be in that crib until he's a teenager," he sighed.

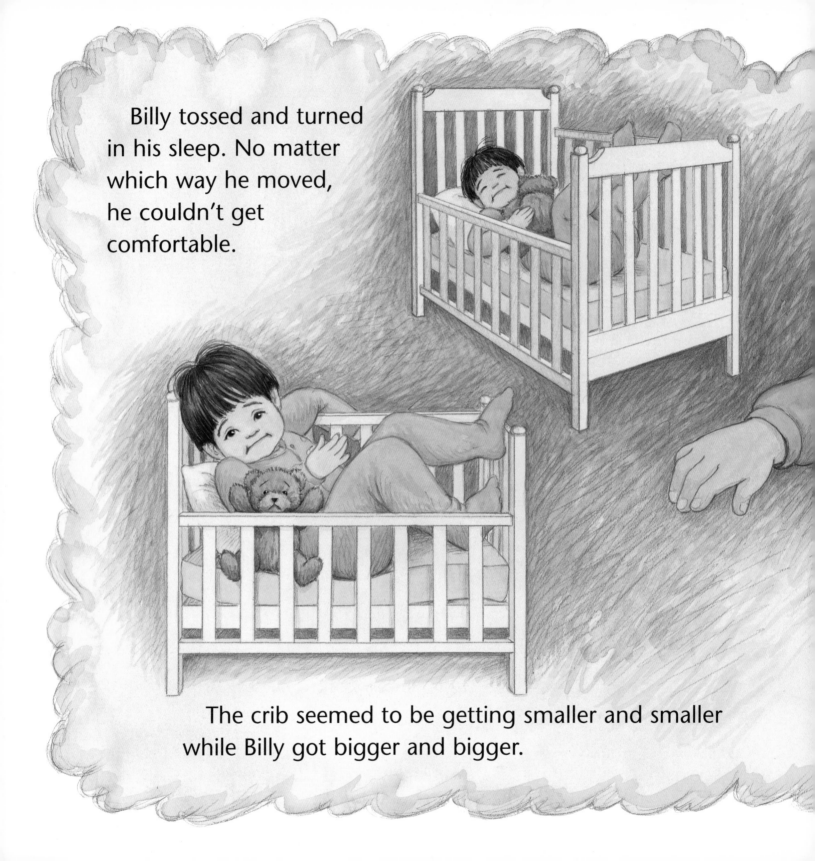

Billy tossed and turned in his sleep. No matter which way he moved, he couldn't get comfortable.

The crib seemed to be getting smaller and smaller while Billy got bigger and bigger.

Fuzz was getting squished. He jumped
overboard to join the other teddy bears
in the big bed.

Early the next morning Billy's mother peeked into his room. She quietly called his father to come and look. Under the puffy quilt in Billy's big-boy bed was Billy, fast asleep with all his bears.

Billy woke up and rubbed his eyes. He saw his mother
and father smiling at him.

"Looks like a big boy slept in his big-boy bed last night,"
said Billy's father.

"Fuzz missed his friends," said Billy, with a proud grin.